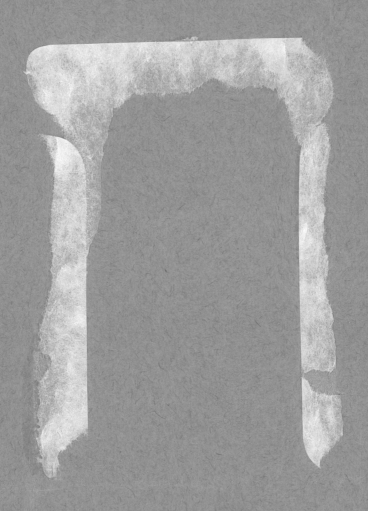

snail,

where
are
you?

by TOMI UNGERER

HARPER & ROW, PUBLISHERS, NEW YORK, EVANSTON, AND LONDON

for URSULA

Books by Tomi Ungerer

RUFUS

EMILE

ADELAIDE

CRICTOR

CHRISTMAS EVE AT THE MELLOPS'

THE MELLOPS GO DIVING FOR TREASURE

THE MELLOPS STRIKE OIL

THE MELLOPS GO FLYING

snail,

where
are
you
?

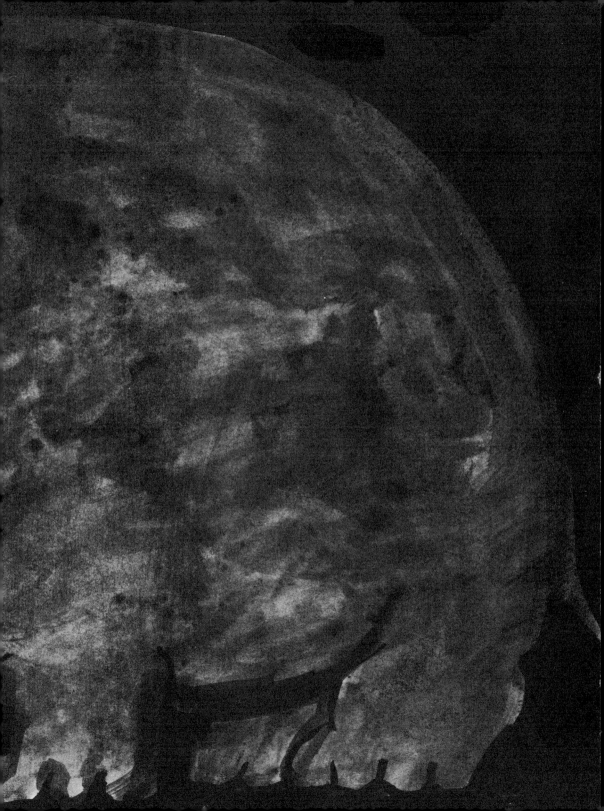

Snail where are you?